Short Stories in Verse

A book of Poems that are more like short stories and consists of some Humorous, some Tragic and some hopefully Inspirational and an element of good cheer hopefully includes something to brighten ones day or cause thought provoking responses.

Owen Robert Cullimore

Copyright 2011

Index

Page

3	Old Doc Taylor
5	My LIttleLinnet
7	Snow Whites Arrest
9	Old Timers Lament
10	The Cemetary Mole
14	The Vicar of Blueberry Cross
18	Little Jimmy
22	Mummy's Bump
23	A Place Called Loose Chippings
26	Grandad land
27	Life on the Trail
30	Little Archie
34	McCafferty's Wish
38	Maria
41	Nurse Mary
44	Old Jack
47	Old Aunt Sally
50	The Aerodrome
53	The Colonel and the Memsab
56	The Down and Out
60	The Sheriff of Horse Manure County
64	The Captain's Wife
67	Abraham
69	The Shepherd
72	A Bad Day at the Bank
75	The Stranger
78	Santa's Bad Day
82	An Unusual Christmas Eve
86	Grumpy Mr Brown
89	Clarence
92	The Dico Lothario
95	The Fractured Todger
98	The Gazunder
100	Dear John
103	Dear Daddy
106	The Little Gothic Shop
109	Little Tommy
112	The Workhouse
115	The Duck That Couldn't Swim
117	A Soldiers Fate
120	The Derby and Joan Club Riot

Old Doc Taylor

Many years ago in Redwood as a boy and a man
I'll tell you this story as fast as I can
About a remarkable person, really special in fact
Who made up for the townsfolk, everything they lacked
He was the town Doctor
Saw through many fears
Helped raise the town
For three score and fifteen years
Delivered all of Mrs McCarthy's babies, fourteen in all
removed Mr Brown's gallstones, whilst he was lying in his hall
Brought over two hundred children into this world
No wonder his hair was grey and tightly curled
Walked everywhere to somewhere, never drove at all
Winter, Spring, Summer and Fall
Always at hand for verybody's needs
Just could not help but do people good deeds
I remember when the Pox took many lives away
But old Doc Taylor, he saved the day
No thought for his own safety, always around
With a kind word and his medicine abound
Most people could not pay, but he didn't care
To serve all his days, always to be there
That was his life, no time for romance
Married to the community, had no second chance
Miss Betty his secretary, loved him no less
Always nearby, in a pretty dress
Though he never noticed, she did not seem to mind
She knew the real man, one who was so kind
During the war, when he left to serve
Fought for his county he had a lot of nerve
Saved many a soldier, thanks to him many came home
It was down to Doc Taylor, they will still able to roam
Came the great winter of thrity-nine or so
Many were left stranded caught out in the snow
But Doc didn't worry, he was still content
Fighting the elements , if people needed him , so off he went
Came the night of the great blizzard, whole town buried alive
A miracle at all anyone survived
Everyone was saved, except one who was lost
Alone, out in the Snow and the Frost
Three weeks later as the great thaw came about
people could move, get out and about
But down by the mill, under a blanket and the dirt
We found Doc's frozen body, he looked so sad and hurt
Frozen to death, out helping others
Tears were shed by us all, brothers, sisters and mothers
This great man had given his life for ours
Trying to help in the end, taking medicine and flowers

To old Mrs McCarthy,having number fifteen
the bonniest baby you have ever seen
She called him Johnny, after the Doc
the man who helped raise like a shepherd will his flock

My Little Linnet

Born in 1900, many years ago
Crippled by Polio, always been slow
Dear little Alice, sunshine four foot six
But with other children, not allowed to mix
Sent to the workhouse, Mum and Dad deceased
her disability became worse, as the pain increased
at thirteen or so, nobody knew for sure
Abused and beaten, no hope of a cure
Old Randall the Bailiff, in charge of the place
took pity on Alice, and her sweet little face
His wife Jenny, a mother of six
Saw to it that she became part of their mix
Despite the calliper on her right leg
She'd walk the best she could on her other peg
Other children would laugh, she would if she could
She only wished that they understood
What her life was like, as a cripple and all
How hard it was for her, to climb the stairs in the hall
Life wan't easy, but she always smiled when she could
Despite her difficulties, she was always good
One day some travelling players came to entertain
The homes residents, they had nothing to gain
Only the joy of brightening the life
Of poor souls trapped in drudgery and lifelong strife
While practising their show one Monday in May
Alice wandered in and started to say
Can I sing for you please, just for to show
That I can do something different you know
Jed the minstrel said why not my dear
Thank you kindly sir, what would you like to hear
Taken aback, not thinking she would know
much of a song to include in the show
Alice stood before them and sang a song
And she warbled her little tune, it didn't take long
To realise something special was happening there
She had the voice of an Angel, it mellowerd with care
With tears in their eyes all gathered round
To hear this young girl, this amazing sound
Stood all alone in her tattered old dress
Dirty and ragged, her hair in a mess
When she had finished everyone cheered
She smiled and walked slowly, then dissapeared
Back to her room so dingy and damp
No wonder she suffered so badly from cramp
Old Randall and Jenny with tears down their face
Took her away from that wretched place
To live with them and their children, good schooling given
So as to nurture her singing, till ten years and seven

As the years passed by, her fame grew and grew
Hers was a name that everyone knew
The little waif had grown into womanhood and more
Sang in theatres and homes, many for sure
But life in the workhouse had taken its toll
Her lungs were a problem to our lovely young doll
Found it hard to breath, at times so severe
It was a suprise to many that she was still here
Her fame had spread widely, far across the land
People travelled miles, just to hold herhand
And to hear her sing, her angelic voice so clear
No one knew sadly, that her time was near
The King even deceided to hear for him self
This young woman so full of musical wealth
So this one evening late in mid June
Up stands this little Linnet, so as to sing him a tune
Throughout the performance, though struggling at times
To breath in harmony with her singing, though not with her lines
At the end the King stood up and applauded with glee
So thrilled at this Angel, he'd been able to see
Alice went to bed for the last time it would seem
In the morning people were left with just a dream
Of their Angel so special, such a gift from above
who had know very little, of life and love
Her funeral was awsome , hundreds attended
She never new, how many she had befriended
At St.Peter's Gate they will be waiting for her to arrive
Always to them her voice will still be alive

Snow Whites Arrest

The names Thursday – Fred Thursday
L A's finest detective
He roams the streets fighting crime
Can't afford to be selective
Called to a stakeout way down town
Some broad called Snow White
Was making powder, or so we thought
She had little guys working all through the night
He and Travis his sidekick
Sat outside the house
Watching, waiting silently
just like a little mouse
At 10.00pm these little guys
Came out, got into a Black Cadillac
Off they went, so they followed close
Each had carried a small light pack
Pulled up outside a disused mine
Hey Ho someone shouted, as they all jumped out
What were these little guys about
The cops waited patiently until dawn
When out they came at last
Off they went back home again
Driving pretty fast
Get on the horn, backup needed
They knew the broad had lied
Once inside we kick in the door
Police, no one move they cried
Sat around the table, they all looked surprised
What the hell do you want Snowy shouted
Ok lady – this is a bust
So wheres the snow we know you've touted
Are you mad came the reply
From some guy called Dopey Red
We've all been down the mine all night
And now were off to bed
A brothel as well whatever next
Thursdays face a picture to see
Thought he'd cracked his biggest case
Known all around he would be
He made a grab for Snow White's arm
Not a very wise move from he
Happy's shovel connected withThursday's head
Stars he began to see
Pandemonium exuded , as Travis observed
A Rottweiler suddenly appeared
Its teeth attached to Thursday's groin
A vivious scream was soon to be heard

Snow White now crying, made for the door
Help she cried in vain
Now loaded into a black and white
Would she be seen again
At the precinct, Lieutenant Frisk
Said I can't believe what I hear
This is Mrs White, who runs the homeless shelter
She's just a lovely old dear
All was well that ends well
The moral plainly clear
Never jump to conclusions
And make Thurasday's mistake I fear

Old Timers Lament

He sits by the fireside in the old Travellers Crest

A pub that he frequents when he needs a drink and a rest

So he can coggitate all the events of his life

The pain and the suffering, trouble and strife

With hearing now faulty, deaf in one ear

Eyes misting over, wetting his beer

Arthritic kness that click into place

Which show up his age like the lines on his face

His sexual conquests a thing long since past alas

A limp looking todger that has since been put out to grass

No longer the bird puller he used to be

Now the only crumpet is the one he gets for his tea

A quiet pint of beer his only true friend

One that will remain with him until the very end

Constipation and Prunes the order of the day

Otherwise he will be in a bad way

Such is life we hear him say

Tomorrow hopefully will be a much better day

But it never is, never fear

It has not been his whole career

Visits to the Doctors to put cream on his piles

And to the Hospital regularly which means walking for miles

Draws his pension weekly, thats all thats left

Without it he would be, broke and bereft

His old black and white tele went out with the Arc

And his insomnia ensures he is up with the lark

Old Mrs Bucannan, at number twenty-tree

Always was inviting him round for a cup of tea

But as he's got older and more miserable she gives him a wide berth

Which might also be down to his much wider girth

No longer the slim Dandy he used to be

His excitement now limited to a nice cake for tea

 Once a great dancer, so light on his feet

Now more like an Elephant, just fat and indiscreet

 He smiles at the ladies as he passes them by

But they ignore his good mornings as they just pass him by

The Grandchildren think he's an old fart

Who sooner or later will be carried away on a cart

And they can share out the money he may have in his piggy bank

Up in the loft by the old water tank

But un-beknown to all, he has been a wise old bloke

And turned the tables on them just for a joke

He been visiting a brothel down Princess Street many a day

And with some of the ladies , having his wicked way

Can't take it with you he thought to himself

So went about spending his ill gotten wealth

Visits the Bookies in Windover Lane

And watches relentlessly his money dissapear down the drain

His wife sadly passed away a few years ago

And never felt the need to bring a new wife in tow

Happy with his own company down at the Pub

With a pint of Guiness and a pork pie for grub

The Cemetery Mole

Down in the Churchyard

In amongst the graves so still

Is a little problem

And it makes me ill

A Mole has made his home

In the family plot

As for our feelings

He does not give a jot

Every time I go to tend

The grave with love and care

I am greeted by this mound of earth

So I know that he has been there

He digs away to his heart's content

The mound gets bigger every day

So I am going to have to trap him

Try to catch it in some way

So I will dig a little hole into his mound

And set a trap for him

A passerby walked over

Said what are you up to Jim

Trying to catch this little varmint

Who is causing me such concern?

I have to teach him a lesson

So that he will learn

To leave my family plot alone

Go somewhere else to dig his tunnels

Because all the mounds he leaves behind

Looks like a row of funnels

So I set my trap, and off I went

Home for a good night's rest

Satisfied I had done my duty

To catch this little pest

As I fell asleep, my mind did dream

This little creature with his pick and shovel hard at work all night

Dragging the dirt to the surface in his little cart

So it would be there for me to see at early light

Suddenly there was a clanging sound

As the trap snapped down on his neck hard and fast

Trapped, struggling to break free

But soon to breathe his last

I awoke with such a start

Shouting Oh Lord, what have I done?

I have killed one of Gods tiny creatures

On with clothes and out I run

Down to the Cemetery at high speed

Till I reached the family plot

I yanked on the trap protruding

To see what I had got

To my relief there was nothing there

I must have dreamt it all it seems

My little friend was still alive

Not dead, like in my dreams

I quietly flattened out his mounds

Thought I can do that every day

It can be a special thing between us

A game that we can play

After all what harm was he doing

Tunnelling away

My relatives now had company

And that's how it will have to stay

The Vicar of Blueberry Cross

Our village not far, quite close in fact

A place full of nosey people, most with no tact

Had a happening not long ago

Only a few months or so

It concerned the Vicar, the Reverend Steed

The man who caused this awful deed

Liked the bottle some folks said

But me, not one to speak ill of the dead

But this Sunday in early September

A day many and I will always remember

When the Reverend Steed disgraced his cloth

And the congregation truly vented their wrath

At ten o'clock, the church was full

Expecting a sermon that would be rather dull

Suddenly the Vicar appeared somewhat dishevelled

Looking as though all night he'd revelled

Bleary eyed and hair unkempt

But a real trooper, he did attempt

To climb the pulpit stairs at least

But people's interest had increased

At the sight of their poor Vicar's state

And wondered why he was so late

He staggered one way then the other

And insisted on calling the Verger brother

Once on top he leaned affront

Dropped the Bible in the font

A few loud gasps had been uttered

Oh dam and blast, we all heard muttered

With book retrieved he looked around

The congregation made no sound

Totally shocked in disbelief

As Mrs Brown waved her handkerchief

So as to enquire as to the Vicar's health

He just glared and straightened himself

Unfortunately forgetting to put on his belt

His trousers now began to slip down as he felt

For the hymn book near at hand

For our first, we will sing the Promised Land

As he lurched from side to side

His inebriated state he could not hide

Blasting out for all his worth

The words he knew, right from birth

A Vicar all his life you see

It was all he ever wanted to be

But the demon drink had taken its toll

As his words began to roll

Into incoherent noises and sounds for all to hear

Many shock their heads and said Oh dear

Mrs Maguire off to the side

Had a grandstand view as his trousers slide

To the floor in all their glory

The sight now becoming gory

Seeing the Vicar in his underwear

She began to profusely swear

A bloody disgrace was all we heard

As he fell from the pulpit like a bird

With a crash he hit the floor

As the verger ran through the door

Seeing the Vicar in his repose

Knelt down and was promptly punched upon the nose

Crimson red his cassock white

The congregation stood in shock and fright

As the Vicar and the Verger punched and squealed

So neither man would dare to yield

P C O'Reilly hearing the commotion

Stuck his head in as was his notion

Seeing the rucas taking place

He ran down the aisle at great pace

Little Tommy Smith thought he'd had enough

Of all this swearing and this rough stuff

Put out his leg to step down from his seat

Tripped O'Reilly of his feet

Jumping up he said with zest

In the name of the law, you two I arrest

So off to the police cell they did go

To cool off for an hour or so

The congregation by this time

Had seen enough of this ghastly crime

Filtered out into the Sun

Having witnessed all this fun

The Vicar and the verger now both in the dock

The Magistrate hearing details how they ran amok

Both got ninety days for this affray

And both come out this very day

The moral of this little tale

That makes us all a little pale

The demon drink can get us all

So into the trap please do not fall

Little Jimmy

Little Jimmy is six years old

And spends his life doing what he's told

Despite this, he has no life

Just abused, a life full of strife

All he wants is a little love to come his way

But for what he gets, he has to pay

His mother beats him with a stick

Thrashes him until he is sick

He fell over and banged himself she says

And tells social workers about his wicked ways

So as to get sympathy for her alone

She even hits him with the phone

It's in the cupboard under the stairs for you

After she has beaten him black and blue

He hates the cupboard because it's dark

It's cruelty that leaves no mark

It's the mental torture he has to endure

Every day and more for sure

If he does not reach seven who will care

He thinks, no one cares, who will miss him if he's not there

His father's as bad but uses a belt

And on his back, he has a welt

Left there from the previous nights beating

As in a corner he was left bleeding and bleating

Sobbing tears, so all alone

He wonders if he will ever be full-grown

How much longer can he take?

This life so cruel and no mistake

He need not have worried he soon knew his fate

As one night his parents came home late

After leaving him locked in his dingy room

With no light on in the dark and gloom

Both were drunk had a few too many that night

And went into a rage when they switched on the light

They saw what nature had made him do to himself

And they beat him senseless with a shelf

Neighbours heard the pitiful screams

It woke them from their peaceful dreams

Someone called the Police, who soon arrived

But it was soon to obvious that Jimmy had not survived

As his life had ebbed away

All his spirit could think of as they took his body away

Was, why me what had he done wrong

To deserve this fate, destiny had it right all along

Social Workers, family and definitely his father and mother

All to blame in one way or another

No one heard his cries for help it seems

Those piercing, blood curdling, desperate screams

How many more Jimmy's have to die

Before someone starts to ask why

Our system fails so many children in this plight

Despite the failures', never give up the fight

Jimmy's parents now in prison where they deserve to be

It's a Childs right to live life free

From abuse of any kind

To those looking on it is a state of mind

So when you hear that dreadful noise, so heartbreaking

Another Jimmy his soul someone is taking

Pick up the phone, ignore the risk to yourself

Just remember that another parent could be using a shelf

With Jimmy gone and his parents locked away

We should ask what is wrong with this world of ours today

That these dreadful situations still exist

Carefully hidden in everyday mist

Mummy's Bump

My name is Sadie

I am five years old

And would like to tell you all about

Someone you would not know

Because she is my mummy

And has been all my life

She helps my stressful Daddy

Cope with all his daily strife

But lately my lovely Mummy

Has been getting fatter, day by day

I tell not to eat so much

To help keep the calories at bay

But for the last nine months or so

Her tummy has got big

And now when she walks off down to the shops

She waddles like a Pig

My Daddy say's we are expecting

A really happy event

And then he and Mummy

Will really be content

It has something to do with a new baby

A brother for me I think

But I don't think this is good for me

Because boys always never wash, pull hair and generally stink

At least the boys at my school do

They tease me till I cry

So the last thing I need is this new arrival

How did it happen, oh why oh why?

Today something strange happened

Mummy became a raving lunatic

She screamed out loud and boy did she shout

An ambulance took her and daddy away, she must be real sick

To the Hospital, when they got there the Stork was supposedly late

Daddy said it must have got lost flying overhead

Does he really think I am stupid, Oh how irate

Why did mummy not have the baby the normal way instead?

Apparently the nurse told me later

Mummy swore at Daddy saying, never again

Don't you ever touch me?

And she raged a lot about being in pain

And when my brother did arrive

Nine hours later, apparently

While I was at my Nanny's house

Having jelly for tea

My Daddy had passed out whilst he was being born

My Mummy cried with joy

And now I have to live my life

With a brother, a nasty smelly boy

A Place called Loose Chippings

Some ways up the road

Not too far away

There is a village I pass through

With a strange name I would say

Loose Chippings it called

A pretty little place

In the summer there's flower boxes

That stands out in your face

Such is their beauty

A Rainbowistic sight

And the street lights shine brightly

At all times of the night

Helped by the glowing

Of the bright shining moonlight

As you drive through

Rarely is anyone seen

Except Old Bob and his dog Bessie

Who is running free on the village green

The local pub sign swings gentle

In the mid-day breeze

And the only sound heard sometimes

Is when old farmer Brown's cow gives a sneeze

So as you drive slowly through

As the other roadside sign says

You will remember Loose Chipping

For the rest of your days

Grandad land

Grandad land is a place like heaven

Where one can disappear

Shut out all the daily noises

A place granddad holds so dear

Where women talk in silent voices

And the kids are rarely seen

We are spared the great indignity

Of being called geriatric, senile, or unclean

It is a place that time can pass

So blissful, serene and quiet

Away from the nagging and the incessant chat

And any impending family riot

The world where Rainbows shine every day

That wonderful place only he can know

So when you see Grandad looking vacant in a chair

That's where he is, so now you know

The Greenhouse or Garden Shed

His main place of refuge when

He needs some space to be alone

In peace and tranquillity once again

He has selected hearing

For those moments which he cares for less

And occasionally you have to wonder

What planet he's on I guess

But he will always still be Grandad

The one who will always care

As he smokes his fag and sits and dreams

In his old comfy chair

So spare a thought next time you see

That he's drifted into his own world to get inner peace

Because when he awakes he will always say

What, when, who of course I was listening, wonders will never cease

Life on the Trail

Hi, my name is Tom Morgan

A cowboy of note

With my old battered hat

And my weather-beaten long coat

I have ridden the range

For almost fifty years

A life full of laughter

Along with some tears

With two trusty colt forty-fives

That hangs down by my side

And they have come in pretty handy

As I have ridden far and wide

My fellow cowboys and me

Have travelled many a mile

Throughout our lifetimes

With good cheer and a smile

Trail herding steers

A few thousand head at a time

Over thousands of miles

In the dust and the grime

Sleeping out under the Moon and the Stars

My faithful horse Old Blackie and me

Covered up in my blanket against the wind and the rain

And with Steers as far as the eye could see

Always on the lookout against rustlers and the like

Waking up with a stiff back and a fart

Looking forward to reaching the end of the drive

Heading straight for a bath and fun with a bawdyhouse tart

Though life was hard in the saddle

My backside sore day by day

Many an adventure was had

In a sad kind of way

Rounding up strays, that had a mind of their own

Or fighting off Indians gone bad

All of that hard tack, bacon and beans did us no good at all

And the loneliness at night rather sad

But I had always wanted to be a cowboy

Since I was a child

Ran away from home at fourteen

I was restless and wild

Got into a gunfight at the age of eighteen

With an outlaw named Bad Jack McGraw

But my hands were faster as I went for my guns

I beat him hands down to the draw

You never forget the first time you kill another man

No matter how bad he might be

As the bullets quickly ripped into his chest, body oozing life

All I could think of was stopping him killing me

Though it was a fair gunfight

He had drawn down on me first

From that sad afternoon

I was forever cursed

As being the man who had killed Bad Jack McGraw

Now known as the fastest gun alive

I disappeared into the shadows settling for life on the range

So as to have a better chance to survive

Because there's always someone faster, quicker on the draw

Your life can be cut very short have no fear

And I wanted to live more than anything else at eighteen

Not killed by someone's six-guns you might hear

So I took up a cowboy's life, found me a reliable horse

That's how me and Old Blackie got acquainted you see

Now we have been together for many a year

Against the world just him and me

Now we ride the range, inseparable, always together

Against the elements we struggle, the heat and the rain

But though our life is hard and full of excitement and danger

We live it daily, again and again

Little Archie

Little Archie Straighton

Twelve years old at best

Took on a morning paper round

You never would have guessed

But one morning bright and early

One dark December morn

At a time when Archie got out of bed

With the rising of the crack of dawn

So to the paper shop nice and early

To start an early round

Carrying his large bag of papers

Through the streets making nary a sound

With his skinhead hair cut

And his bovver boots on his feet

With a attitude for a twelve year old

Who lived mostly on the street

 But no thug was Archie

He was just following the current trend

Most of his friends dressed this way

No harm did he intend

But this fatefully December morning

Whilst walking up Old Mother Baileys drive

To put her morning paper through the front door

Down past her old Bee Hive

All the Bees were agitated

Flying around in a swarm

The air was beginning to fill with smoke

Her front porch felt rather warm

Looking through the letter box

Archie saw flames were blazing down the hall

And lying at the bottom of the staircase

Was Mrs Bailey, obviously having had a fall

Poor Little Archie's dilemma

Racing through his head

Did he run to town and raise the alarm

Or break in the door instead

Realising the seriousness of the situation

And that to wait may be too late

He kicked the door, which flew open with a crash

And ran in, he did not hesitate

Grabbing Mrs Bailey

With all the strength his little frame could raise

Dragged her down the corridor and into the garden

Out from inside the Smokey haze

As Mrs Bailey regained consciousness

Started shouting for her grand-daughter Flo

Who was apparently asleep in an upstairs bedroom?

So back in the house did Archie go

Dousing himself with water

With the hosepipe attached to the side of the house

Dashed back inside and up the burning stairs

Faster than any mouse

In the distance could be heard the ringing

Of a fire engines bell ring belting out

It flew up the narrow lane

Pulled up with a screech and a fireman gave out a shout

Mrs Bailey by now was well with it

He's gone back inside she loudly cried out

As suddenly Archie appeared at a window with the baby

Threw it open shouted you will have to catch her, look out

Three firemen held out a blanket as Archie quickly let the child drop

They caught young Flo, now in a shawl she was wrapped

Who was now saved from the blazing inferno?

But little Archie was now inside trapped

As the flames burst out of the windows

An explosion was soon to be heard from inside

And the roof now had began to cave in

It was plain to see that little Archie had died

A braver hero you would never have encountered

The townsfolk all said for many a year

Mrs Bailey could never look at her granddaughter

Without shedding many a tear

The little cottage has now long gone

Replaced, by a bright shiny plaque

In loving in memory of their young hero

Who lost his life, will never come back

If there is a moral to this little tale

It's never judge a book by its cover, don't get caught

By a skin headed boy in his bovver boots

Who was not the tearaway everyone thought

McCafferty's Wish

McCafferty walks from his park benches

Dressed in his coat left from the trench's

A relic from the Great War, which he managed to get through

There amongst the muck and bullets, one of the surviving few

Many friends are dead and gone

His life he feels just lingers on

No one knows and no one cares

As on the streets he sells his wares

Wears fingerless gloves to keep out the cold

His face now parched shows he is old

Craggy face that rarely smiles

Feet are blistered through walking many miles

Trudges the street in search of shelter and food

People sometimes help if there in the mood

Most times goes without its true

Though he may be down and out he is never blue

He has his friends the Squirrels and Rabbits

In the park with their funny habits

Sleeps under the stars, his private covers

Lies quiet still doesn't disturb the lovers

Makes Pegs and Matches which he sells

Even if he sometimes smells

His hygiene leaves a lot to be desired

Caused mainly from being forever tired

On street corners he plies his trade

Selling items that he has made

Today he has got three and six

Feels as though his life is playing tricks

Has enough for a bed at Mo's

Some soup, a bath and a change of clothes

Feels like an Earl or a Lord at least

With sixpence left enough for a feast

As the day draws in he's about to leave

When he feels a tug upon his sleeve

A little waif about six or seven

Who looks as though she is bound for Heaven

Spare a copper for some grub

She says as her eyes she gives a gentle rub

Taking pity McCafferty says

Young lady, we have both seen better days

For different reasons I'll be bound

Says she avoiding a passing hound

Aye that's true I'll give you that

He replies looking at her little hat

Come my dear we will dine tonight

Amongst the stars that shine so bright

So spending all on food and water

To give to Alice, for tonight, his adopted daughter

For the night she would tag along

And to his surprise she would sing a song

Her sorrowful tale she did recant to him

Which hit him hard, upon the chin?

When she had eaten and drank her fill

He thought she looked so kind of ill

Laid her down upon the bench

Her face the colour he had seen in the trench

Settling down amongst the stars

His neighbours being Jupiter and mars

Drifted off, cuddling his child

Who asleep just looked so meek and mild

On waking Alice was still where she had slept

But in the night the grim reaper crept

And took her away to pastures new

To the place reserved for the chosen few

A priest was called who took her body away

McCafferty was left to rue the day

Which had little meaning to his tomorrow

His heavy heart was filled with sorrow

That night while back amongst the stars so bright

A lady in white appeared during the night

Be not afraid I mean no harm

I am here to work my magic charm

People who know and care have seen

What you did for little Alice Dean

I only did what I believed was right

McCafferty said scared by the sight

Do not be afraid she spoke so soft

Make a wish she said holding her hand aloft

I wish for Alice for no more to be afraid

That's all I would like to be paid

For my kindness to that little girl

With her blonde hair and falling curl

I am a poor sinner, no hope for me

Just go away and leave me be

Falling asleep he just drifted off

Only to be awoken by a passing moth

Rising early he made his way

To the spot where people pay

To buy his wares, on this fine day

Something happened, in a very strange way

He sold all his goods, never known before

As though someone had opened a special door

His life changed forever from that day

Now he no longer needs to stay

Out amongst the Stars, but he still sees his friends

It's nice to think that's how it ends

Maria

Maria is from Croatia a far distant place

How she arrived here is such a disgrace

Dragged away from her family at only eighteen

With a promise of a life she had never seen

Coming to a position that would pay well

And keep her in clothes and send money home as well

So as to help her parents who were quite poor

And the money she would send would help them more

Put on a plane and arrived in the dark

Taken to a house that was quite stark

Raped and abused by many men

Never thought she would see home again

Made to work as a prostitute twenty-four seven

In dark and dingy rooms taking money she was given

Many a beating she had to take

Otherwise, her body would end up in a lake

Her body now battered her private parts torn

No longer had need of the dress she had worn

So often used didn't know the time of day

I wish I were dead was all she would say

Sold on three times for a few thousand pounds

To further deprivation as bad as it sounds

The treatment the same, more rape more abuse

Forced to work in massage parlours, what was the use

Frightened and lonely and at her wits end

She was lucky that one client became her friend

He arranged her escape, helped her to flee

But she still never knew how safe she would be

He got her to a safe house, many miles away

Now hounded by police who wanted help in any way

To stop those responsible, close their evil trade down

And make the streets safe in the city and town

Maria was lucky in the end she was saved

But would always be wary, alone and afraid

She could no longer trust anyone she would ever meet

Always apprehensive when out in the street

The Rapes and the Beatings her body abused

Deeply disturbed though not alone still confused

How anyone can survive such an horrific ordeal

The pain and the suffering is hard to conceal

She grew up as a young girl full of laughter and fun

Despite being poor, her life had begun

So these promises of a better life were welcome for sure

To help her poor parents, to give them more

Her illusions shattered, what's left for her now?

She has to learn to cope with the pain somehow

But someday she will meet that special man

Who will truly love her and help her all he can

Not all men are as evil as those who abused

Her trust and naivety for which she was used

What hurts her most is her inner feeling,

Her body's no longer her own, it will take time healing

The thought of someone being sold, used and abused

Is against all humanity, leaves one aghast and confused

How could countries let this happen, why no deterrent

The anger it raises, makes one incoherent

Something must be done to stop this evil trade

So people must be made aware, not kept in the shade

Maria had rights, which were just ripped away

But at least with help she lives to fight another day

So don't bury your head in the sand

Raise up your voice and give Maria a hand

To raise awareness of this evil trade

Of selling young girl's bodies and the money that's made

No thought for the minds and souls that have been taken

Leaving bodies mangled, abused minds disturbed and shaken

Just remember it could be your very own daughter

So don't wash it under the bridge of life, just like flowing water

Nurse Mary

Mary is a district nurse

She travels round each day

To see her patients, give them the care they need

As she wends her merry way

She has her trusty bicycle

Which is nearly as old as she?

But it lets her peddle for miles and miles

So she is as fit as fit can be

In her basket which fits upon the front

She carries all she may need

And she can be seen by every one

Travelling around at her own speed

There's Mrs Maguire at Appleton Court

A saintly woman of means

But her health is not what it should be

And when Mary calls her face just gleams

To see someone so caring

Who looks after all her needs?

And to while away the time and make some tea

And bring happiness, she always succeeds

Old Mr Partridge at Apple Road

Who lives alone now his wife has passed away

Who is a miserable old so and so

But who Mary still calls on every day

She cooks and cleans but he still moans

The world need's putting to right

He complains he needs more money from the state

To pay for his television and his heat and light

Saint Mary listens, but has problems of her own

Which intermingles with her own woes?

Being recently diagnosed with cancer

But she feels that's the way it goes

So she must grin and bear it

Still thinks of others before herself

Has no one at home to turn to

She is a spinster left on the shelf

Married to her profession

Always putting others first

And as usual in life for caring people

They always come off worst

But Old Molly Catapult

A name to conjure with its true

Said it must have been a shot in the dark

Because her family were a motley crew

But Molly loved her garden

Where flowers bloomed all year

And Mary used to help her weed it

They enjoyed doing it together never fear

But as time went by Mary's health became worse

She began to get tired more quickly than before

And when twilight time is near at hand

She is glad just to get through her own front door

But this particular morning she never arrived at all

No smile for Mrs Maguire, or any of the others too

Mrs Catapult felt so all alone

She did not know what to do

But she contacted the local policeman

Who called to see if Mary was all right?

And after breaking into her cottage

Found she had passed away that night

All her friends were saddened by the news

Her patients most of all

But they all knew how ill she was

And the reaper would someday call

And now in the memorial garden

Just away up the road from the infant school

They have erected a memorial garden

With a Plaque and ornamental pool

Because Mary was the person

On whom all the village could rely

And would be remembered by all that knew her

And even those who passed it by

The work that someone like Mary does

Is sometimes never really appreciated to the fullest extent

Until the day they are no longer there, then it becomes so evident

Old Jack

Old Jack was a hobo

A man of no means

Who spent his life looking in old Dustbins?

Eating stale bread and beans

Some days he might be unlucky

He had good days and bad

But to him life was free and easy

Some of the best times he'd had

But the worst time is the winter

Sleeping on his bench in the park

Just a Times newspaper

To keep him warm in the dark

When the Snow came in 69

A bad year all round

Even he wondered that winter

If one morning, dead he would be found

Bur surprisingly, his old army great coat

Was so thick and warm, comforting too?

People would recognise him immediately

And say how do you do

He travelled the roads

The kings highways no less

With his belongings in a swag bag

And his old mongrel called Jess

His faithful companion

For many a year

Together they had been roaming the district

With a smile and good cheer

But the sixty nine winter

Did them no good at all

They were in trouble

The minute the first Snow did fall

Trying to shelter

Under the bench in the park, just they two

Poor old Jack was near death

And Jess was too

But this particular morning early, before first light

The Reverend Peabody

Was walking home this dark night

He had been late at the church

Wanting to be home before daylight

Seeing the stricken two companions

Freezing to death in the Snow

He awoke the two wanderers

And home with him they did go

Once inside the Vicarage

With a raging hearth fire on show

Settling in quietly with some tea and some cake

And old Jess lying in front of the fire

What a scene it did make

Soon both fast asleep

Off to bed the Vicar did go

Whilst the our two trepid explorers

Slept through the worst of the Snow

In the Morning bright and early

Just before dawn

Both jack and Jess

Awoke with a yawn

About an hour later

The Vicar came down to make some tea

But all he found was an empty room you see

Both jack and Jess had taken their leave you see

But had left a note

Thanking the vicar for his kindness to his hospitality

But they had not wanted to be a burden

On him or society

So back on the road

Refreshed and with a spring in their gait

To enjoy the open road and to wander

Before it was too late

Thanks to the Vicar's kindness

They both had a new lease of life

To think someone had cared

About their suffering and strife

So always remember

A good deed will bring happiness

So never pass by, when someone is in distress

Old Aunt Sally

On the corner of the street

Next to the Haberdashery shop

Near the newsagents where dad gets his papers

Where I walk with him and skip and hop

There lies old Sally's Antique shop

That sells all sorts of brick-a-brack

Aunt Sally can sell you anything

She really has the knack

All sorts of wares are on display

Mainly junk it looks to me

But I love when Dad takes us in there

It's like Aladdin's Cave you see

Its seems to go back through the shop

For miles and miles to a little one like me

As I walk amongst the things on show

There's such a lot to see

One day I spied an old Rag Doll

Alongside a Teddy Bear battered and worn

And I asked my dad if I could take them home

Holding teddy's arm which was badly torn

Brought memories flooding in

Of a child in the war walking the street

Holding him by the arm

I wonder what happened to that child

For now in my toy room he will go

And I will make him a coat

Fill the holes with stuffing

Because I really love him

That's a fact I thank my dad

But late that night I was half a sleep

I swore he was singing

And moved but the song I never knew

I tried to tell dad

But he said what a strange imagination you have

Over the days when I went out to play

I visited the haberdashery to say

Do you know where the bear came from?

Aunt Sally I asked but she was wondering where my dad was

All she could tell me in the end

It belonged to the boy in a great big house

But he had been killed in the war

And the song I heard was his favourite as a child

So on this day I plucked up the courage

And knocked on the door

There stood a man ten feet tall

Hello can I help you he said

So I explained but when he saw my teddy tears ran down his cheek

Little girl you are so sweet

Christopher loved this bear

Like pooh did his honey he would not part from it

For love or money

But on the day he got killed

I couldn't stand to see it

So in Aunt Sally's shop it has been buried

And now a young girl has made him like new

I'm so pleased for you

You can bring him in for tea

But did you know he sings

But like magic he stops

Because grownups can't hear

Just special children with a gift

Did you buy the rag doll as well?

Be careful she has magic powers

You see my son was a magician

With magic spells

He would play for hours

With his talking friends some alive some dead

So be careful when you wish

It will sometimes come true

The Aerodrome

One Christmas Day morning a few years past

The Fog was quite thick, and was closing in fast

Took my dog Buster, a Golden Retriever, one of the best

To the old Aerodrome a few miles west

Parked off the road, just by the gate

7 am in the morning, did not want to be late

For the day's festivities, with the family and all

Hopefully a day full of merriment, have a real ball

So out of the car, and off we went

Striding out well, morning felt heaven sent

Fog getting thicker and a real eerie feel

Wrapped up warm against the early morning chill

Walking on the runways now long past their prime

Out in the Fog, it was like returning in time

You could feel the drone of the planes in their time

Feel the presence of the airmen all in their prime

Out of the gloom, a figure appeared

Dressed kind of funny, it really felt weird

In flying suit, helmet, large boots and a jacket

Out in the mist the planes were making a racket

Though startled for a moment, I swiftly said hello

He looked at me strangely, I thought he would go

But he smiled and said Hi, my name is Joe

I am an American Airman, but I guess that you know

I nodded my approval, we shook hands and we talked

Said he came from Kansas, related more as we walked

His piercing blue eyes lit up the gloom

His infectious smile would brighten any room

Said he was married, just wanted to be there

With his wife and children, sat in his old rocking chair

Though only twenty, he looked a lot older than that

I noticed the frown from under his helmet hat

The lines on his face truly said it all

How hard life was now trying to save us all

Suddenly I was startled, by something he said

He missed them all greatly, now that he was dead

He looked at me caringly and just shook his head

Said sorry for disturbing me, it just filled me with dread

I looked straight ahead, dumbfounded at best

Thought I had better go home, I need a rest

As I turned back to face him, he was no longer there

Just as he had come, he disappeared into thin air

I thought I was dreaming, just called Buster

Said nothing to no one, left the situation alone

My curiosity was raised by something he had said

About being in a churchyard and something I had read

About an American Airman, killed in the war

Now I was intrigued, wanted to know more

So I went to the local Library, dug out some books

There on a page, my airman's good looks

Staring up at me, I found it hard to believe

So more information I set out to retrieve

It seems he had died in his plane that had been his plight

Flying over Southampton, one dark night in a dog-fight

His body was found and buried nearby

No one to mourn, no one to cry

Family so far away, lost forever it seems

Now he's just a memory, part of their dreams

I will always remember a chance meeting at best

With a poor soul we needed, now hopefully at rest

The Colonel and the Memsab

As they sat on the veranda of the Hotel Exotic

Drinking the old G & T

Between reminiscing their lifelong romance

And the occasional hot pot of Tea

Old Colonel Maguire, of the old Forth-Fifth

The regiment now long disbanded

To listen to his tales of gallantry and battles fought

You would have thought he had beaten the Fuzzy-Wuzzies, single handed

During their time in the Sudan, under Kitchener I believe

Leading his regiment into battle almost daily

But Mrs Maguire, now well past her prime

Just smiled a lot and ranted quite gaily

As they talked about things from so long ago

When he was a dashing lieutenant, so daring and brave

And she looked so radiant in her best Sunday dress

In those days men knew how to behave

An officer and a gentleman was the order of the day

No bad language, not a hair out of place

The Memsab in turn, at his side everywhere

Travelled along at her own steady pace

When a dashing young officer, named Captain O'Rourke

Took a fancy to the Memsab, so elegant and beautiful she did look

Fisticuffs ensued the night at the Kings welcoming ball

The like, of which you only find written a book

A few raised words of the jealous kind

And a slap with a glove, accompanied with the threat of a duel

As things get mightily out of hand

With the Memsab lighting the fuel

The Colonel and O'Rourke squaring up on the lawn

Like two prize-fighters ready to do battle

For them nothing unseemly as pistols at dawn

No sound of a flashing Sabre's rattle

The Memsab, just watched, smiled and then turned away

Leaving the Colonel to do what he thought was his duty

To defend his wife's honour, good name and all

Against a Captain who had got a bit fruity

After a few punches, and blood running noses

No Pistols or Swords anywhere in sight

Te altercation was quickly dispersed

And everyone disappeared in to the night

Such was life in the old Regiment

Everyone was upright and true

The old colonel with his stiff upper lip

Whose language frequently turned the air, blue?

But the Memsab, still as pretty as she was in her youth

Her tight dress still caught the men's eyes

But by now age was catching her up

Along with the heat and the flies

But still together, and so much in love

Holding hands, with still a spark in their eye

Together seemingly forever

Or was that spark just a sty

The Down and Out

As he awakes to greet the dawn

On his park bench amongst the dew

The Times newspaper he has used for a blanket

The one read by the chosen few

As he stretches out his arthritic arms

And moves his arthritic legs

His eyes now staring up at the rising Sun

As he drinks from his cup, now full of dregs

He greets the day with his usual smile

Though the garden he surveys is owned by the city

As people pass him by and tut

He resents their look of pity

I may be a wanderer he thinks to himself

But self respect I have so much

I need no one's indulgent stupid remarks

I do not need society's crutch

As he makes his way to who knows where

Each and every day

Spending his days on the road and free

Searching for food along the way

Every dustbin is his restaurant

Each titbit or morsel that he might find

Will keep him alive and independent

He is just the roving kind

Each night he returns to the municipal park

His bench is always there

Another newspaper will keep him warm

So he can sleep without a care

But he is not alone it seems

He has a field mouse for company

Who arrives each night to sleep in his pocket

And will even partake a sip of his tea

As he sleeps he must remember

Not to turn over or disaster could strike

He would crush his little rodent friend

The one he has nicknamed Mike

So together they settle beneath the stars

Out in the cold and rain

And when they awake they both need to rise

And face the world again

Old Roddy, our gallant hero

From fighting, on the Som, in world war one, and yet

Has memories that bring him nightmares

Of things he saw that he would rather forget

Time has passed him by so much

His mind a blank to the person he once was

No one knows a thing about his life as they pass by

The ones who glare and cuss

But he always greets the day with a cough and a smile

Puts newspaper in his shoes to fill the holes

And watches intently as the old park-keeper

Clears up the work of last night's Moles

As Mike runs off to forage for food

Old Roddy prepares to venture out into the morning Sun

Because his greatest adventure is about to rise

Unbeknown to him it has begun

Because every day is a new beginning for him

Where he will travel only he knows

But he will always return to his park bench home

In the park where the flowers grow

So if you pass him by asleep

Or if he is awake just say hello

Because unlike him you surely will

Not have far to go

And just remember one thing

When you see Roddy out in the rain and snow

He and his little field mouse friend Mike

Have nowhere else to go

His pockets may be empty

His clothes may look like rags

And as he wanders around the place

His worldly goods are all in bags

But that does not make you a better person

Than he ever could have been you see

But for fate and misfortune

It could be you or me

The Sheriff of Horse Manure County

Back beyond Deadwood

A lot further north

Lies the town of Brittle Creek

For all that its worth

It has a real problem

So many horses passing through

And so much horse manure

They don't know what to do

The streets are disgusting

Can't tread anywhere

If you venture out

Just have a care

They have even tried blocking

Horses rear ends with a cork

Till one exploded

When stabbed with a fork

To keep the streets clean

Just to alleviate the smell

Needed to clean up the sidewalk

It was a real living hell

Old Duster the doctor

Had a son named Ben

He was into chemistry

Blow's up now and then

But he has an idea

To retain all this methane gas

Made from the horse's manure

And it came to pass

He persuaded the Marshall

The Mayor and the rest

To build an incinerator

So he could put the theory to the test

To filter the excrement

From the horse's rear ends

Into a form of power

But that's not where the story ends

The filter plant was built

At the south end of town

Young Ben in his element

But seeds of disaster, had been laid down

Everyone was commandeered

To clean the streets well

All offending matter removed

So as to keep the place looking swell

The plant was now working

Employing quite a few

Ben's reputation

Just grew and grew

Street lamps were provided

Lit by the gas

Made from the shortcomings

Of a horse's arse

Everything was ok

Until one day in the fall

The pressure had built up

But no one noticed at all

The boiler exploded

Oh what a mess

Town covered in brown liquid

Looked bad, I must confess

The stench was deplorable

Smelt for miles it would seem

A brown town in the wild

It looked just like a bad dream

The Sheriff now suntanned

Well that's what I thought

But he was spitting blood

As young Ben he had caught

Wanted to lynch him

Leave him for dead

For covering everything

In manure it was said

But old Judge Parker

Who was rarely sane, more like dead?

Came to the boys rescue

Gave him thirty days instead

So that's how the town

Of Brittle Creek was renamed

Now known as Brown Creek

And now you know why it's famed

The Captains Wife

She walks the corridor at midnight

The lady with her lamp that shines so bright

Looking for the lover she lost

That sad and painful night

Skipper of the lifeboat

That went down with all hands

Found smashed to pieces in the morning

On the Cornish sands

Went out that dark and stormy night

To a vessel in distress

Trying desperately to save as many lives

A terrible situation I must confess

The waves they were enormous, fifty feet or more

It was no wonder they were smashed to their deaths

Against the rocky shore

It was six o'clock in the evening

When the distress call was received at the lifeboat station

With no fear or apprehension for their own safety

All the gallant crew soon leapt aboard the Atlantic Nation

The lifeboat the men had served in, for more that fifteen years

But this stormy and desolate night no one realised it would all end in tears

Approaching the vessel in distress

Four people were seen on deck

The boat now battered and sinking

It was a broken wreck

Expected to sink any moment

No time to lose, hold fast

Came the cry for the Lifeboat Captain

Watch out for that falling mast

The mast crashed onto the lifeboat

Just as a mighty wave was seen

Approaching from the starboard side

A fifty foot wall was on its way, really mean

The lifeboat and stricken yacht crushed together as one

No one survived the tempest; the sea's work was done

Only the wreckage left to tell the tale

Just a mangled remain and a small piece of sail

Mary the wife left worried at home

Anxious to get her Captain and his crew safely back ashore

Had to wait till morning for the bad news to reach

That all hands had perished, would come home no more

As the bad news was received everyone wept

At hearing what had happened as safely they slept

For all of the monuments, for of the praise

Did not stop Mary wishing the days

When she and Mathew were together as one

Their life of laughter, passion and fun

Now midnight was never welcome, brought memories back

So alone she would wander, as love she did lack

Her man gone forever, along with his crew

So weeping and roaming was all their was left to do

Many years later, as time went by

Mary found happiness with another guy

But always in memory of her man and his crew

She never forgot that night the sea raged and blew

Though love has returned into her life

To her she would always remain a lifeboat Captains wife

Abraham

Abraham was a young boy, just sixteen years of age

Ran away to join the Army which was all the rage

Lied about how old he was, should have been eighteen or more

But no one really cared; they just let him in the door

So off to France he was sent to fight

Marching away out into the night

Never knowing in the reality that had just begun

He would one day fail to see the rising Sun

Life in the trenches, was dire and hell on earth

But he fought for King and Country, always for all his worth

Mortars and Grenades fell near to fill him with dread and fear

All he could think of was those he held dear

The Mum and Dad he had left behind

Not daring to tell them what was in his mind

To fight for his county, to make them proud

Not to return home under such a cloud

One day being injured with his colleagues by a mortar shell

All he remembered was the pain and the yell

Of dying soldiers now lying in the trench

The blood and guts and the terrible stench

Reporting to sick bay they said you're alright

Get back up the lines because you're fit to fight

Another Grenade then fell close by

Now well disorientated he began to cry

Found wandering aimlessly alone in the mire

Still enduring the fear of the enemy fire

Taken to headquarters court marshalled for cowardice they said

He not realising he would soon be dead

Tried and convicted by those in charge was he

Forgetting how totally scared and innocent he might be

To die by firing squad was the decision

Only years later to be disbelieved and treated with derision

The Shepherd

An Angel appears out of the mist

The trickling stream just now Sun kissed

A beacon in the morning dew

Awakens the stillness that God threw

Over the Mountain and down the Valley

How many times before only he can tally

As she smiles her radiance does elegantly bloom

To lift many a lonely Shepherds early morning gloom

As he watches his bleating flock with care

He never notice's that she is there

Keeping him out of harm's way

To help him make through the day

This lonely soul on whom others have lent

To bring them milk and supplement

Their meagre lives, harrowing at best

Life is hard for him and the rest

But his beliefs will guide him through

His Lord will show him what to do

A saint full man who gives his all

To his flock so they may not fall

Into danger on the Mountain high

As he whistles and gives a sigh

To appreciate the life that he has received

From his Lord, what he has achieved

His spirit never bending or broken down

Though living miles above the town

People know him as Adam that's all

No second name that they recall

He walks the Mountains with his flock

Never bothering to take stock

Of the words that others may

About his life he lives his way

The solitude and peaceful existence

Has brought about stubborn resistance

To a life in the valley below

What he reaps he will sow

The sheep just wander here and there

As if they know they have no care

They are always safe from harm

No need to be upon a farm

As he goes about his daily life

The Angel watches him through the strife

Of bad weather and other dangers lurking

Unaware he continues without shirking

His duty to his Lord and flock you see

His faith a comfort and will always be

Forever to roam for a million years

No time for pity, no time for tears

The Angel watches, listens and takes stock

Of the Shepherd and his flock

She knows that her presence he always feels nearby by

Though he cannot see her and she knows why

He's been dead for a hundred years or so

His flock disappeared long ago

But the Mountain he refuses to leave

To go to Heaven, not to grieve

His duty to him is quite clear

By his sheep he must be near

Only ever seen by the chosen few

Wandering amongst the early morning dew

A Bad day at the Bank

Mary was a teller at the local bank

Took in the money as you she would thank

For calling to see her behind her till

But suddenly she stood quite still

As on this day a robbery took place

A gunman came with stockinged masked face

Firing his gun into the air

Gave all and sundry quite a scare

Threw his bag onto the counter top

Fill it up quickly just don't stop

Or else you get it was his yell

Hurry up or I'll give you hell

Mary, frightened did as she should

Fearing he would shoot her, she knew he would

Put the money into his black holdall

But some notes to the floor did fall

Pick those up he did roughly shout

As he turned to glance at his lookout

Who was outside in the getaway car

Which they needed to escape far

Firing his shotgun into the ceiling

This immediately had everyone reeling

Diving for cover onto the floor

As his accomplice ran inside the door

Screaming, the Police are all around outside

We have no place to run and hide

Mary had pressed the panic button behind the door

Just as everyone was hitting the floor

A five foot Teddy Bear was on display

The prize for the banks raffle, by the way

The gunman realizing they were in trouble

He grabbed the teddy at the double

Anyone moves this guy gets it he ranted

With the bear as hostage the seed was planted

For a long standoff, or so he thought

But the police just wanted the robber caught

Racing for the door with the Teddy Bear in tow

Being used as cover for all we know

Don't shoot someone said the bear could get killed

So the police put down their weapons, as around their cars they milled

Sargeant O'Hara a policeman of note

Took out a revolver from under his coat

Took aim, fired, what a loud din

Shot off the Teddy's arm what a pickle were in

A lady pedestrian saw the commotion

As the bears arm was shot off, oh what a notion

She collapsed on the pavement, oh God, what have you done

Just as the villains cut loose with a shot from their gun

Sergeant O'Hara quick as a flash

Across to the villains he did quickly dash

One flying leap both were brought to the floor

We give up they cried, we don't want no more

Grabbing the Teddy to a very loud cheer

Minus one arm sadly I fear

He was hailed a hero but that was not all

He got a medal for bravery beyond the call

No one realised quite what had taken place

But the Chief Constable really had a red face

To think that his men had been fooled one and all

Into thinking a Teddy Bear was real made him feel small

The story in the papers, good reading it made

How a lone police officer had put the rest in the shade

He understood what it was all about, sometimes all is not what it seems

And that Teddy Bear's are only real, in our imagination and our dreams

The Stranger

A child all alone and feeling forlorn

Dirty, hungry clothes all torn

Lying in an alley trying to sleep

Fighting for survival, his life to keep

Stranded and abandoned, his life on the streets

He's just glad that each morning he greets

The Sun as it's rising and able to breathe life

Although another day of heartache of misery and strife

As he huddles up closely to keep out the cold

He wonders if ever he will grow old

The danger he faces each day of his existence

He meets head on with lots of resistance

But this night would be different than the rest

Though to see him asleep, you would never have guessed

As the rain and the wind whistled down the street

He wrapped himself up and covered his feet

The pain of the hunger, barely able to stand

There across the road people were eating grand

He could see them in the distance, not far away

But could only watch an in the end just pray

As the Snow started to lie on the ground

He pulled his covers all around

So as to help keep out the cold night chill breeze

And to avoid the lasting freeze

As he drifted away to another place

A deathly white was on his face

The elements trying to claim another child

This inclement weather so cold and wild

From nowhere a hand did just appear

Rested on his shoulder to allay all fear

Come my son the stranger said

Let's get in the warm and find you a bed

Awaking from his deathly state

Meekly awaiting his final fate

The hand felt warm and reduced his fear

Of having this stranger, now so near

They walked away together; he was not sure how far

Almost run over by a passing car

The Stranger never said his name at all

And the boy so weak, he did almost fall

As they approached a Hostel the Stranger said

Go through the door you will find a bed

But I have no money the boy replied

That's not needed just go inside

As the Stranger held out his helping hands to say goodbye

The boy noticed scars in his palms and wondered why

He had those round marks embedded deep

This Stranger who saved from his final sleep

The man remarked that's the suffering caused by others fear

A price I paid so very dear

And the scars around my head

Caused by others wanting me dead

But never fear I did survive

To help keep children like you alive

The boy looked at the door and began to walk in

If felt warm inside on his freezing skin

He looked back to thank the Stranger but he was no longer there

Bewildered he closed the door, he didn't care

He was now safe and was given a bed

Where he could lay down his weary head

When he awoke he looked around

Nothing stirring, no earthly sound

But above him mounted on the wall

Was a Cross known to one and all?

It was the Stranger that he recognised from his hands

Nailed to the Cross in far distant lands

Now he knew why his friend was scarred and had been hurt

And he cried for forgiveness for the lesson he had just learnt

Many years later when a grown man

Whose life since that night had gone to plan?

The one someone had mapped out for him

That dying boy, so weak and thin

Never knowing that night who the Stranger might be

Now all was clear and he could see

The Lord had sent his son to watch over those in need

A lesson in faith was learned indeed

Santa's Bad Day

Every Christmas is just the same

For poor old Santa Claus and all his friends

All hard work and sleepless nights

And a feeling of heartache that never ends

Will they deliver all the toys on time?

And make all the children's dreams come true

So their working around the clock

No time to slack, that will never do,

The little elves are full of fun

Now all the work is under way

The lathes are turning, all that noise

It's the start of another long, busy day

Rudolph awakes from his peaceful sleep

Shakes the other Reindeers awake

They have to polish Santa's Sleigh

What a sparking job they'll make

On the benches partly made toys

Plans for new ones by the score

What a lot of chattering noise

Deciding who does what, to make some more

Santa cleans his clothes, must look his best

Always aware of whom he might meet

While he travels on his delivery quest

At any house, on any street

The days pass by all hard at work

The elves all joking and sometimes curse

They have no time to sit and shirk

If they fail to deliver they'll feel worse

But Santa has a problem looming

His suit is missing, nowhere to be found

How can he to the children be zooming?

Someone has stolen it, I'll be bound

Now the search is on in earnest

Can the suit be found in time?

Everyone is searching and full of zest

They really have a mountain to climb

A black cat is spotted outside looking in

This one brings trouble by the score

The wicked Witch has she been near

If so the suit could be lost for evermore

The Witch hates Children and Santa Claus

And will hurt them all she can

By stealing Santa's bright red suit

It's such an evil plan

She intends to burn it in her cauldron

And recant some evil spells

Hocus Pocus and all the rest

In the smoke and vile smells

Leg of Toad, hair of Rabbit

Some Deadly Nightshade too

All gets thrown into the pot

As she stirs her thickly goo

But Peter the Pixy and Alf the elf

Have caught on to her evil plan

So of to the Witches lair they go

To get in as soon as they can

Climbing through an open window

Down the stairs to her cellar room

To find her book of spells

And cast her to her doom

As she recanted her evil spell

By the fire where her cauldron heated

Both Peter and Alf we well aware

She had to be defeated

Grabbing her spell book quietly

They began to read

They found the one they needed

Which would turn her into seed

When they were spotted, the Witch turned in a rage

Cursing and shouting, to stop them was a must

But they were two quick, and into the cauldron went the page

And saying the spell, she just turned to dust

Finding Santa's missing red suit

They went hotfoot to the grotto as quick as they could

And the look on Santa's face when he saw what they had

Now the children presents could be delivered just like they should

Once all the presents were delivered there was a great sigh of relief

And for years he has remembered, the memory would stay

How the old wicked Witch had tried to ruin Christmas

And how Peter and Alf had saved the day

An Unusual Christmas Eve

The Holly hangs on the old Church door

Ever open, ever sure

To take in the homeless at this Christmas time

At six am the bells do chime

To let people know that someone's around

And it's where shelter can be found

For those Hungry and Homeless, in deep need

Away from those so full of greed

Who do not care about their fellow man

And never think of others when they can

I'm all right jack, does for those

They have their food, drink and clothes

That someone may be dying through lack of food

Doesn't spoil their festive mood

Selfishness, sad but true

But not for the likes of me and you

The Christian spirit still shines through

Some of us know what to do

To help the needy at this festive time of year

Like the Reverend Brown his task is clear

His Church always has an open door

For those in need and many more

In his Cassock standing proud

His booming voice so clear and loud

He has a withered, damaged right hand

Injured whilst helping his fellow man

In the trenches in World War 1

Serving as a medic at Verdun

The sights he saw, long remembered since

Of pain and suffering that made him wince

In the suffering, bullets and muck

In his mind the images stuck

So he now devotes his life to giving grace

Far removed from that desolate place

Where he saw so much death and destruction

Now to the followers of Jesus he gives instruction

But one lonely Christmas evening past

He though that he would breathe his last

In his church a solitary figure in black

Sat in the pews, three from the back

When Reverend Brown past the time of day

This is what the stranger had to say

Pulling a gun he boldly stated

He wanted cash his eyes looked elated

High on drugs the Reverend thought

So he had better do as he aught

But the man started crying, softly at first

Complained profusely that he thought he was cursed

That he had been in trouble since he was a child

And all his life on him the pressures had piled

With his gun hand shaking put it up to his head

And told the Reverend he wished he were dead

The man of the cloth, now feeling sad

Tried to comfort the man, tell him he wasn't bad

But a victim of life, that sometimes deals a bad hand

And he wasn't the only one in our fair land

Give me the Gun the Reverend said as a command

The young boy looked up; put the gun in his hand

With his hand on his shoulder the reverend spoke

Just as through tears the boy started to choke

Sometimes young man we lead our own destiny

That's what tonight has brought you to me

Because you need a helping hand, from the Lord don't you see?

So trust in him, me and Jesus to help set you free

But Reverend tonight I have gravely committed a sin

Don't worry my son, salvation comes from within

You have just made the first move, by giving me the gun

And you're now on the road to redemption, so follow the Sun

Will you call the Police the young man now enquired?

Looking so sad, forlorn and downright tired

No said the Reverend you will be ok

Because I think a lesson has been learned today

That you're not so alone as you plainly think

Having these feelings that lead men to Drugs and to Drink

You are not the first and you won't be the last

Because you see in this world the die has been cast

But never forget that you're never alone

In God's heart you will always have a home

So pick up the pieces, go out in the world and face

All that it deals you, there's no better place

Grumpy Mr Brown

Mr Brown lives in Easy Street

Not far from my house, just a few feet

The most miserable man you have ever seen

You always are aware just where he's been

Upset all and sundry down through the years

Had many a neighbour reduced to tears

His wife a very amiable soul

Sometimes wishes she could disappear into a hole

Having to watch and listen to the entire goings on

Would have had a breakdown before too long

If it were not for little Tommy Smith and his Chemistry set

So read on and the better it will get

One bright morning in early May

Just around eight, the start of his day

Mr Brown was at his front gate

When a neighbour walked by obviously a bit late

Out walking his dog a German shepherd bitch

Named Princess, who barked, sending Brown into the ditch

A list of expletives followed swiftly

To which the neighbour reacted niftily

An argument ensued, the usual thing

A row with a neighbour had a familiar ring

The dog took a snap at Mr Browns behind

Missed said Mr Ratcliffe, Oh well Princess never mind

Mr Brown, now in a foul mood

Who always claimed he was just misunderstood

Walked off down to the privy at the end of the garden at the back

Swearing and snarling, in a mood that was black

Little Tommy Smith from his bedroom window he watched

And a cunning plan now was about to be hatched

With Gun Powder from last bonfire nights firework remains

And some of his dad's fertiliser and some Gas from the drains

He loaded it all in a canister tight as a drum

Now a lethal weapon it all had become

So he would wait for his moment to get his revenge at last

For Mr Brown confiscating his catapult one evening past

So a few days later on a Sunday very early I think

Tommy crept into the garden, through the fence that had a missing link

Planted his incendiary device in the privy out of sight

Went home smiling and waited for the daylight

The morning started as usual, with another row, as was the norm

And then off to the privy went Mr brown true to form

Shut the door behind him and went about his ablution

Tommy Smith watching closely in his hand he had the solution

A press of a button, and a very loud bang ensued

Off came the roof, the door and in the nude Mr Brown now stood

His trousers round his ankles, now all surrounded by smoke

A cough and a splutter, Oh dear did he choke

A ragged shirt was lying on the floor

The toilet paper had followed the door

And was now flying up the garden at a devastating rate

Being pursued rapidly by the toilet seat that stopped at the gate

Mr Brown's face now covered in black dust

Tommy Smith had his camera, a picture was a must

He now had his revenge, satisfaction for all

Everyone rejoiced that Mr Brown had a fall

The sight of this man who had made peoples lives' a misery at best

At this moment in time not one neighbour cared less

They were so busy laughing at this sight for sore eyes

All that could be heard were the neighbour's satisfactory cries

That's how little Tommy Smith became the hero of the day

That unforgettable time in early May

As for Mr Brown he never knew

Who had caused his misfortune to this day its true?

Clarence

Clarence the Parrot an African grey

Always had a lot to say

Bugger this and bugger that

Expletives even worse hurled at the Cat

Where he learnt them, no one knows

But I suppose that's how it goes

But his owners wanting to cure him of this affliction

Wanted him to learn good diction

So of he was taken to the Vets for salvation

And to a specialist for a new creation

To be a Parrot with a more amenable approach

So off to Professor Higgins for him to coach

Clarence in a more fruitless vocabulary

But trouble ensued, got made worse you see

Unbeknown to all Professor Higgins himself

Had his own problems despite his wealth

Liked a drink or two while he was working

Said it stopped him from shirking

Kept him going with difficult patients its true

But with Clarence he had no clue

As the work got harder, Clarence was having a ball

No progress made, didn't see eye to eye at all

Getting more frustrated and hitting the bottle

It looked as though Clarence he would throttle

Expletives became more frequent as time went by

From both Clarence and Professor, Oh dear, Oh my

Later that evening consumed by drink

The poor old professor could hardly think

Letting rip with all kind of swearing

As Clarence's presence became more wearing

Slowly they both succumbed to sleep

Both prostrate, not making a peep

Next morning Mrs McCumby did call

To collect her Clarence, all cured and all

So off home she went so full of joy

Just like a child with a brand new toy

Came the night of the party, her friends were all there

Even Mrs McNulty the town's lady mayor

Mrs Johnstone from number forty three

And a few others who usually came for tea

Clarence in his element now cut loose

Swearing and delivering all kinds of abuse

Saying show us your knickers to Mrs O'Malley

And calling Mrs Brown old fat Sally

Mortified to say the least

Mrs McCumby said shut up you beast

Wondering what she had paid Professor Higgins for

All of a sudden there was a knock on the door

Outside in the rain the Professor stood

Worse for drink, feeling hurt and misunderstood

Knowing Clarence was worse than before

He wanted to coach the Parrot some more

Mrs McCrumby now decidedly incensed

Gave him a right hander with such intense

The Professor collapsed on the floor in a heap

Totally sparko, fast asleep

Clarence seeing the activities at the door

Let loose with more expletives, swearwords galore

Most, could not be repeated, in this tale

If they were we could end up in jail

Mrs McNulty now mortified

Sat in the corner and cried and cried

But Mrs O'Malley had her revenge it would seen

Just as Clarence let out a scream

Grabbing her scarf she boldly wound

It around Clarence's beak so he could utter no sound

For the rest of the night he sat on his perch up high

Not able to mutter as much as a sigh

The Disco Lothario

He gets home from work

Had a shower and a shave

Its Friday night

It's time for the rave

So it's off with the denim shirt

He's had on at work all day

And out with the Red Silk one

His pulling shirt he would say

It's into the shower

With his Shampoo and creams

On with Brut and old Spice

The smell's of his dreams

After a shave and a wax

To get rid of chest hair

So his medallion hangs right

And swings through the air

It's on with his trousers

Two sizes too small

And to do up the buttons

He has to lie on the floor

On with his shades

A pair of old Foster Grants

Which have been around

As long as his pants

A quick look in the Mirror

To check all is ok

A leering grin greets him back

Then he's on his way

Jumps into his old Morris Minor

He's had for thirty years

Don't you just know?

It will all end in tears

So down at the disco

He burst's on the scene

The new John Travolta

People wonder where he's been

Out on the dance area

White jacket thrown to the floor

Which a bouncer uses

To block a draft under the door

The disco lights spinning

Ranging down on his head

His bald patch is now shining

And like his shirt, turning red

Sweating profusely

As he dances away to the tunes

Belly hanging over his trousers

Which looks like two balloons

His bald head now shining

Into the D J's eyes

Pop goes a button

Which came from his flies

As the drink takes effect

His dancing becomes more erratic

Flailing his arms and legs

Just can't stay static

Though he's a laughing stock

He doesn't care

Though too old and balding

He's just glad to be there

You're a long time dead

Is his outlook on life

His Friday nights

Relieve his daily strife

Of working in the factory

From seven to seven

Out on the dance floor

He's in his own heaven

He just wants to rave up

As long as he can

And to prove to all the ladies around him

He's some kind of man

The Fractured Todger

Mr Smith a vain and obnoxious man

Overdid it one hot steamy night in June

Making love passionately

Under the Stars and Moon

Disturbed by a very large dog

His partner panicked and wanted to run

Who, leaping up, inadvertently kneed Mr Smith in the groin

Which caused damage he had rather not had been done

So off to the Doctors he did go

With his Todger well and truly bent

Moaning and groaning profusely

His love life suddenly well and truly spent

The Doctors receptionist Mrs O'Reilly called out next

So approaching the counter he meekly did smile

What's wrong with you she said, eyeing up Mr Smith?

Who was groaning and holding his groin all the while

Had an accident, and it got bent

He whispered cautiously not wanting to be overheard

Speak up she bellowed, don't be shy

What got bent, Oh God don't be absurd

But it has he shouted forgetting his plight

With others in the waiting room now listening intently

I've definitely bent my thing-a-ma-gig

It all happened accidentally

A likely story said Mrs O'Reilly

And into Dr Roberts he was sent

Who looked up saw this man holding his groin

And then sat and listened intently to his predicament

Explaining how this misfortune had happened

About making love and being disturbed

Flopping it out onto the table

The Doctor now stared and looked quite perturbed

His Todger was without doubt

Now well and truly bent

Now at angle of forty-five degrees half way down

And lent either way in the position it was sent

Mrs Casey the Doctors new assistant

Who had been the lady in question who caused this mishap?

Screamed Oh my God when she spotted the problem

Lurched forward quickly slipped and fell into Smith's lap

A loud scream came from Mr Smith's person

Who by now was distraught at the sight of his old chap

Now bent bruised and aching

And leaking like an old kitchen tap

The scene was like something from an old farce

Because Mrs Casey had by now slipped to the floor

And hearing the commotion, the racket and row

Mrs O'Reilly was stood in the door

Mr Smith had jumped up

His Todger now waving free in the air

With Doctor Roberts now creased up in laughter

Who promptly fell off his chair

The sight of Mr Smith's anatomy

All battered and bent

He ran out the surgery cursing

No one knowing which way he went

When all gained their composure, a mystified look

Had overtaken the laughter that was rampant throughout

When everyone heard in the surgery

What the fuss was all about

Meanwhile Mr Smith damaged Todger and all

Had arrived back home by Taxi no less

Into the bath for a jolly good soak

How he survived is anyone's guess

The Gazunder

Mrs O'Reilly woke up with a start and the hump

From a noise she heard that made her heart thump

Someone was walking out on the stair

Who she knew should not be there

With her heart racing two to the dozen

Arms were moving but her legs seemed to be frozen

Fixed to the spot, lying in her bed

Her mind now racing, well filled with dread

Hearing the footsteps coming closer out on the landing

There was a squeaky floorboard where the burglar was standing

Knowing she may have to stand and defend herself

She reached under the bed and put the jerry on a shelf

Which incidentally she had used only shortly before

Some of the contents of which fell on the linoleum floor

As the handle of the door was turned into the open position

Mrs O'Reilly became a woman on a mission

No burglar was going to steal the jewels her husband had gave her

The Gold Rings and Silver Bracelets and his Gold Electric Shaver

As the intruder stole through the now open door

She thought I'll teach you to steal from the old and poor

As he crept around the room unaware, she was awake

Slinking and sliding around like a snake

For he had trodden on the spillage that was on the floor

And was gradually moving towards the window by the door

Getting up all of her courage Mrs O'Reilly leapt out of bed

And grabbing the jerry hit the man on the head

With the contents now running all down his face

He started weaving all over the place

Another sound whack and he wobbled a bit more

Staggered and crashed down onto the floor

I'll teach you to break in and steal my belongings she cried

But he dodged the next swipe, and rolled on his side

Leaping up swiftly he made for the door

But Mrs' O'Reilly being nimble hit him once more

The burglar staggered, lurched and fell full throttle

Out through the open window, followed by a bottle

That Mrs O'Reilly kept by the side of her bed

To hold her Jack Daniels, or so her nurse said

Hurtling down to the ground with remarkable speed

Followed by the jerry in which she had just peed

Laying prone on the ground making long moaning sounds

The burglar, was arrested by a Policeman, out on his rounds

Mrs O'Reilly the hero of the day

Along with her gazunder, which had survived by the way?

Dear John

The Teardrops fell upon the note

Of the Dear John letter she wrote

To Mathew fighting at the front it seems

No longer the man of her dreams

Whilst he's been away another beau

Has captured her heart, he has to know

Though she is sad, it must be done

Because on her mind it weighs a ton

As he is fighting in the trenches

No time for thinking of loving wenches

Just to stay alive is Mathews first thought

Not to dwell on news the post has brought

Though it hurts, he can understand

Why she has another man

Been apart two years or more

No longer there to close the bedroom door

To take her in his arms and to have kissed

Those loving lips he has so badly missed

Making love, joined as one

The laughter, tears when they had fun

Now all was gone, no time to dwell

As the shelling started another spell

Of battle raging in the mire

The situation was becoming dire

In between the mortar shells

He wrote back in short spells

It took him time to pen his note

But this is what he lovingly wrote

Dear Mary dearest I understand

I have been away in this God forsaken land

Fighting for my King and Country in these trenches

In with the dead and dying, and the stenches

It must be hard for you to understand

With you back there your life so grand

I am sorry for the pain I have caused by being away

But I expected to return any day

But you have your life and I have mine

Fighting for freedom so I am fine

So I wish you well for the future dear

And now know I will no longer hold you near

But the note he would never sign

As Mathew died shortly killed by a mine

The bloodstained letter was found intact

But never read by Mary, that's a fact

It blew away in the early morning breeze

Helped by a Sergeants loud violent sneeze

As the letter drifted across Flanders Field

It was found years later in some Farmers crop yield

He read it and heartbroken he passed it on

To the military who were now long gone

It now rests in a museum in Mathew's place of birth

As a reminder of the sacrifice made, a true soldiers worth

Dear Daddy

Dear Daddy why did you have to go away

Why couldn't you stay until another day

All those times you held my hand

And tried to make me understand

Why you were sick and looked so pale

Like a piece of bread that had gone stale

The noises you made behind the bathroom door

The day Mummy found you on the floor

The Doctor said you would be ok

You were just not very well that day

Or was that just so I would not know

That your body's resistance was so low

Gone now are those times you put me to bed

And the stories you always read

The jokes you would tell to make me laugh until I cried

Now all that has ceased now you have died

I miss most your loving smile

That seemed to beam out all the while

You were always there to dry my eye

If I fell, got hurt and it made me cry

Mummy's lost without you by her side

Since you have gone, she's cried and cried

I try to comfort her when I can

But I cannot replace her special man

Now were together just us two

Therefore, I do not know what more I can do

So I spoken to God and let him know

That I love and miss you so

So you will always know

What I said and told him so

To tell him he had disappointed me

So this is what I said, was it really me

Dear God why did you let my Daddy die

And make me and Mummy cry

Why couldn't you leave things well alone?

Wish I could talk to you on the telephone

Maybe then, I could put into more sensible a word

Some things you may have never heard

How mean you are to destroy a life

Before its time, and make Daddy leave his wife

I trusted you and you let me down

And to hear you name just makes me frown

My faith in you has been severely dented

So I hope you are contented

My daddy was the greatest man

And even worse, he was your greatest fan

He took us to church every Sunday

And made sure it was a real fun day

So God how could you let this happen to me

No longer to have my Daddy comfort Mummy you see

I just wanted to let you know

Just how much you hurt me so

I have to go now Mummy's calling

As I go, the tears are falling

So you remember what I said to you

Because letting this happen will never do

So daddy as I stand here by your grave

And say all the prayers that I did save

To help you on your merry way

There is so much I want to say

I hope you're not disappointed in my action

Of telling God of my dissatisfaction

But I could not let him get away it seems

With destroying mine and Mummy's dreams

So now, go to sleep with my affection

As now, my life has a new direction

I must look after Mummy help her through

But at nine years old how much can I do

THE LITLE GOTHIC SHOP

Down in the village

In the centre square

Lies a little Gothic Shop

People hardly know it's there

Lanterns swing outside the door

A bell rings as you enter in

You are greeted by the owners smile

More like a cheeky grin

Yes, my dear the woman says

Holding out her hand

Covering each and every finger

With a silver band

Her rings are all unusual

None are very small

One has a little Lion on

She bought it from a market stall

As you look around the shop

At all its wondrous stock

Imagination runs away with you

Just like, you have had a shock

There's Dragons, Wizards and the like

And Incense burning, it smells so right

Witches by the score abound

To some it could be quite a fright

The Dresses hanging in the alcove

Take your breath away

Majestic colours, Red Blues and Greens

In styles that look so gay

Fancy boots, some short some long

With laces by the score

There is even a Highwayman's cloak

Hanging behind the door

On a shelf there's giant's castles

Where Wizards ply their trade

Along with their Frogs and Toads

It's where the magic spells are made

All the unusual Jewellery and Ornaments

Are put out on display

For you to try on and look at

In the hope that you will pay

To take some of it away with you

A dress to wear, a fancy ring

Something that takes your eye

It could be anything

Well my dears the woman says

What can I sell you today?

Can't let you in and out again

Without you have to pay

Her Earrings hang loosely down

Dangling from her ears

Dressed from head to foot in black

A true Goth through and through

Little Tommy

Little Tommy Blenkinsopp

Lived with his mum above the shop

The apothecary in Chapel Street square

Everyone knew his dad's shop was there

All around brought their ailments for him to cure

With his drugs and potions to be sure

A busy place most of the time

Spotlessly clean, free from grime

One day little Tommy was sifting through

Items left for dad to do

Included in the assorted work

Was a pair of teeth to repair for old Mrs Burke

Therefore, Tommy thought he would give dad a helping hand

The best chemist to Tommy in the land

Trying to fix the teeth, he glued them apart

He said to himself that will do for a start

And Mr Wheeler's laxative pills

The ones that supposedly cured all ills

He mistakenly put into Mrs O'Reilly pack

And put them in the store room upon the rack

Dear Mrs.Burke came to collect her teeth and left

So pleased and no longer without them, feeling so bereft

And returned a short while later in quite a foul mood

But Tommy's dad misunderstood

Could not explain what had taken place

And tried not to laugh at Mrs burkes face

Her mouth seemed to be permanently open wide

So bad in fact you could see well inside

Little Tommy looked so sheepish and ran to hide

The game was up, Mrs Burke then cried

As he ran, off down the street

Mrs O'Reilly he did meet

Clutching her backside and obviously upset

And realising a hiding he was going to get

I will kill you she cried, I know it's' your fault you little sod

Swearing and cursing and waving a wooden rod

As Mrs Burke joined in the pursuit down the street for miles

She sounded like a Rottweiler suffering from piles

But little Tommy was crafty, knew how to avoid capture at all cost

As Mrs O'Reilly slipped up on the ground covered in frost

A loud noise erupted from her backside as she hit the floor

What happened next, please don't ask, I implore

As Tommy slipped down an alley and out of sight

He thought I had best go to Auntie's and stays there the night

As Mrs Burke with her mouth still, open wide

And Mrs O'Reilly with her sore backside

Went back to Tommy's dad to try to make sense

Of what had happened, to get cures for their predicaments

In the end, all was well Tommy got the blame

And the next day he had a rear end the was aflame

A jolly good spanking was all he got

But for Mrs Burke and Mrs O'Reilly, an experience they never forgot

The Workhouse

In the year of 1853

So poor, it's to the workhouse for me

No Mum, no Dad no family

I am just another bastard you see

Inside the place it's cold and damp

I suffer ailments, like colds and cramp

Sitting here I feel so forlorn

Beginning to wish I had never been born

Work in the laundry from dawn to dusk

Living on gruel, and sometimes some Rusk

Beaten, starved and they call this home

Is it no wonder I feel so alone

Only ten years old am I you see

I should be living happily

Skipping gaily as a child

A little girl so meek and mild

But here I am so often used

Beaten, damaged and abused

I work so hard every given day

But still get treated in this way

Mr Bartlett runs the home

I think he has a heart of stone

Takes no notice of my plight

Ignores my screams throughout the night

Young Johnny takes such a great delight

In hurting me, this is my plight

Bullies others, just like me

Would tell but no one listens you see

Calloused hands and chilblained feet

As a child I've changed, no longer mild and sweet

I have to steal to stay alive

Or sell my body to survive

Another long day, a sad one too

I lost a friend her name was Sue

Found dead in a doorway, having run away

Starved, half naked some did say

My heart grows heavy by the day

In this place I have to stay

Washing, Ironing sheets and things

Whatever arrives, what the rich people bring

Today I feel so tired, my body weighs a ton

And the day has only just begun

By noon I need to go and rest

To an alcove I know best

Down in the cellar, cold and damp

I lie on rags, behind a ramp

Out of sight, not to be seen

No one will know where I have been

As time rolls by, sleep turns to passing

Another child not everlasting

My name is Jenny, but who cares

Just another orphan living downstairs

The plight of children in these times

Can't be put into nursery rhymes

Sad but true, no one dared

In truth and reality no one cared

For the poor it was the workhouse plain and simple

To the rich, these people were just a pimple

On the backside of society

Not interested in Jenny and where she may be

Another lost soul, no one would miss

Was found early next morning, no one to kiss

Her goodbye, died all alone

No longer in that horrible home

The Duck that Couldn't Swim

Watching by the river's edge

Bright and early in the early morning glow

A female Duck came waddling by

With babies one to eight, into the water she did go

Little ones followed all in a row

Until it got to number eight

Who got to the edge and stopped to wait

Mother stopped and looked around

Little baby making a quacking sound

Come on in, she did imply

Baby shook his head as if to say why

Brothers, Sisters all looked on amazed

As brother on bank just sat and gazed

At the water, not impressed

Had no intention of being pressed

Into the water as mother wanted

This was one request, not to be granted

Dipped his foot into the water deep

Into this don't think I will creep

I looked on bewildered and amused

To see a duck look so un-enthused

Not intending to do as he was told

Though so small, but yet so bold

Back came mother and a chase ensued

Along the river bank I was bemused

To see this duck in hot pursuit

Of her baby who looked so cute

Once caught, mum grabbed him by the neck

Looked to say, you will by heck

Come into the water with all of us now

No time to waste, learn to swim somehow

Into the water the mother duck went

Full of parental good intent

Put her chick onto the water, who suddenly reared

Went up, went down and disappeared

Panic stricken mum dived down

Grabbed her son who was about to drown

He was panicking flapping his wing

And just as suddenly began to swim

Off he went across the water fast

Mum and remainder followed at last

Down the river they all swam

Out of sight down by the dam

I walked off slightly mystified

To see a Duck that nearly died

But all was well, it ended fine

They all swam off, all in a line

A Soldiers Fate

As I sit her contemplating my life

Gun loaded just like a dice

Enemy approaching like a blanket of destruction

As I sit here covered in fleas and lice

Another night in the trenches

More worry and more woe

Feeling a little bit downhearted

Not knowing whether the end will come or go

Must cheer up my comrades

All dreaming of home

Not needing to be here

Nor wanting to die alone

Cannon fire sails over

It's just begun

More noise and destruction

At the rise of the sun

Stay alert is the order

Hold fast, don't give ground

Search for my tin helmet

Whilst I fire another round

The scream of horror

As someone has been hit

More blood and guts

Just lands in our pit

Families back home

Have no idea

The pain and suffering

We have to endure

Officers are no different

All scared just the same

They just give orders

Someone else is to blame

The enemy advances

We have to hold out

Bombs keep exploding

Around and about

I must have been hit

Deep pain in my chest

I spin around quite sharply

A large hole in my vest

Crimson tide starts running

My life ebbs away

To die here my destiny

What more can I say

As nightfall approaches

My body is still

Will not see tomorrow

Dear God, They have broken my will

To live any longer

Just can't stand the pain

Please close my eyes gently Lord

Whilst a sinner you gain

The Derby and Joan Club Riot

Sitting in this cell

With deep regret

After a night

I will never forget

With thirty others

Pensioners one and all

Our night of excitement

The yearly ball

Arrived at seven

Me and the wife

Looking for laughter

All we got was strife

It all started happily

Everyone was on form

Apple Punch flowed freely

As was the norm

But jealousies were evident

Between some of the wives

A few single men

Could cause such a surprise

Old Mrs Bailey, a vicious old hag

Not nice at all, looks had long been lost

Became upset at remarks made

So revenge at all cost

Put Gin in the Punch

With some Vodka and Wine

Suddenly lots of laughter

Not a good sign

The music was playing

Dance floor was full

Women swirling, their dresses full blown

And the single men on the pull

Old Mrs Brown, not used to strong drink

Was flailing about as the bright light flickers

Let it all hang out, she was having a ball

Fell on her arse, showing her knickers

A scream from the band stand

Come help me please

Old Mrs Riley

Was down on her knees

The drink had awoken

Desires long forgotten

Tried to debag the singer

Oh dear, how rotten

Old Mrs Smith, with revenge on her mind

Picked up a custard pie, she had spied with one eye

Spotting Mr Davies

Taking good aim she let fly

He ducked, saw it coming

The Vicar not nimble or fast

Caught it smack in the face

All were aghast

A punch up ensued

Could not believe my eyes

All these demure old ladies

Throwing these pies

Fisticuffs abounded

All were involved it had strived

Someone dialled 911

The police then arrived

There was total disbelief

On Sergeant Brow's face

Women were fighting

All over the place

Chuck them in the wagon

He yelled with great force

Off to the cells, we'll arrest them all

The judge can deal with it as a matter of course

On Sunday the vicar

A bit worse for wear

Went to his pulpit

High in the air

The disgusting behaviour

 At the Derby and Joan

Had caused him great concern

And boy did he moan

Authors Profile

Owen was born in Reading in 1945 and moved to Ramsdell in Hampshire when he was two years old which was a Public House and a Small Holding with a number of Cows and Chickens, a situation which has been a constant source of information for themes, situation's for his writing.

In 2004 he met his long lost sister Linda Bevan who was a poet and since then they have shared their love of writing together producing books of Poetry as well as Children's Story Books.

He is married and has three Daughters and lives in Hythe, Southampton with his wife Gillian who also acts as proof reader to ensure the best quality book is produced.

All the poems are based on thoughts and creations from the mind be they from actual events, Imagination, Dreams or just pure fiction that has been created from nothing.

Hopefully the reader will derive as much please from reading this collection of Poems as the writer obtained from creating it